HORSE IN THE PIGPEN

HORSE IN THE PIGPEN

By Linda Williams

Illustrated by Megan Lloyd

HARPERCOLLINS*PUBLISHERS*

To my children, Patrick,
Nicklaus, and Samantha
–L.W.

To the Miller family, with special thanks to
Beth, Madison, and Schuyler for being such
great models. Baa Hurrah!
–M.L.

Horse in the Pigpen
Text copyright © 2002 by Linda Williams
Illustrations copyright © 2002 by Megan Lloyd
Printed in Hong Kong. All rights reserved.
www.harperchildrens.com

Library of Congress Cataloging-in-Publication Data
Williams, Linda, date
Horse in the pigpen / by Linda Williams ; illustrated by Megan Lloyd.
p.   cm.
Summary: A child tries to get her mother's attention as chaos erupts around the
family farm.
ISBN 0-06-028547-8 – ISBN 0-06-028548-6 (lib. bdg.)
[1. Farm life–Fiction.   2. Mother and child–Fiction.   3. Stories in rhyme.]   I. Lloyd,
Megan, ill.   II. Title.
PZ8.3.W679255 Ho   2002   00-032043
[E]–dc21   CIP
                                                                                        AC

Typography by Al Cetta
1 2 3 4 5 6 7 8 9 10
❖
First Edition

H<small>eeey,</small> M<small>a.</small>

Horse is in the pigpen, rollin' in the slop.

Tell it to the pigs, dear. It's time for me to mop.

Heeey, Ma. Pigs are in the chicken coop,
peckin' at the grain.

Tell it to the hens, sweet.
My ring slipped down the drain.

Heeey, Ma. Hens are in the doghouse,
gnawin' on a bone.

Tell it to the dog, hon.
Grandma's on the phone.

Heeey, Ma. Dog is in the bunny hutch,
hoppin' up and down.

*Tell it to the bunny, love. Auntie's come
from town.*

Heeey, Ma. Bunny's in the cat bed,
playin' with the yarn.

*Tell it to the kitty, dear.
I've five more socks to darn.*

Heeey, Ma. Kitty's in the duck pond,
swimmin' on her belly.

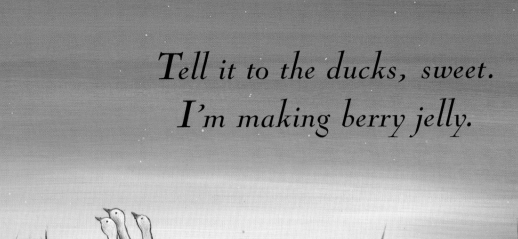

Tell it to the ducks, sweet.
I'm making berry jelly.

Heeey, Ma. Ducks are in the cow barn,
wearin' Daisy's bell.

Tell it to the cow, hon.
My angel cake just fell.

Heeey, Ma.
Daisy's up in my bed.
I'M SLEEPIN' IN
THE BARN!

Heeey, NO! Go and fetch the broom now!
I'll straighten up this farm.

Heeey, Ma . . .